ONCE I WAS A PLUM TREE

ONCE I WAS
A PLUM TREE

Johanna Hurwitz
illustrated by Ingrid Fetz

William Morrow and Company
New York / 1980

Library of Congress Cataloging in Publication Data

Hurwitz, Johanna.
  Once I was a plum tree.
Summary : Increasingly aware of the differences between her family, who are nonobservant Jews, and their Catholic neighbors, 10-year-old Gerry Flam begins to investigate her heritage. [1. Jews in the United States—Fiction]
I. Fetz, Ingrid. II. Title.
PZ7.H95740n [Fic] 79-23518
ISBN 0-688-22223-4
ISBN 0-688-32223-9 lib. bdg.

Printed in the United States of America.
1 2 3 4 5 6 7 8 9 10

For Nomi and Beni,
new branches on an old tree.

Contents

1
A Long Day in September

Why are parents so inconsistent? One day we had bacon and eggs for breakfast, and the next day my mother said I couldn't go to school because it was Yom Kippur. That is the most important Jewish holiday of the year, and suddenly my parents remembered that we were Jewish. We weren't Jewish enough to go to a synagogue. And we weren't Jewish enough to fast (that means not eat any food all day), which is what other Jews would do on Yom Kippur. And we weren't Jewish enough to stop eating bacon for breakfast or pork chops for dinner (which Jews aren't supposed to eat on *any* day of the year). That morning I said to my mother, "If we aren't observing Yom Kippur, then it isn't really a holiday for

9

us. So why can't I go to school with my friends? It doesn't make sense to stay home."

"Geraldine Flam, I've already told you six times," she answered. "It wouldn't be nice to go to school. Your grandparents would be upset if they knew." That didn't make any sense either. After all, my grandparents would never know. They were dead.

So there I was, sitting alone on the stoop outside my house on a Wednesday morning; all the other kids on the street had gone off to school. That made me different. On my street in the Bronx, almost everyone was Catholic, and they all kept busy observing their religion. My best friends, Ann D'Amato and Patricia Quinn, both had made their First Holy Communion. Every Tuesday they attended religious instruction, and every Friday they ate fish. They went to church every Sunday. They knew just what to do and when to do it. I wished I was Catholic like my friends. In my family, every day was the same. We might call ourselves Jewish, but we never did anything special to prove it. Instead of feeling Jewish, I just felt different.

Mostly, my parents said we were American. My ancestors came to this country almost 100 years ago. During the First World War, my grandfather changed his German-sounding name from Pflaumenbaum, which means plum tree, to Flam, which has no meaning, to show that he was truly American.

Once my mother's family had been observant Jews. But my grandmother died when my mother was born, and my grandfather stopped believing in God that very day. The Flam family were Reform Jews. That means they could eat or do whatever they wished. I think they were practicing how to stop being Jewish. But my father always stayed home from school on the holidays. When my parents got married, they decided not to bother with the business of religion. They said that they didn't believe in all those old traditions and superstitions anyway. "We are assimilated," my father explained. "We fit into American life like everyone else," he said. But still they wouldn't let me or my little sister Lyn go to school on Jewish holidays.

So there I was, sitting on the stoop, not fitting in at all, but rather sticking out like a sore thumb. I felt like a nothing, just like my name. I wondered what my grandparents would have said, if they could have seen me there on September 24, 1947, spending Yom Kippur on that stoop.

I seemed to spend an awful lot of time sitting there. I bet if I added up the time that I'd sat there, either talking or playing with Ann and Patty, it would have been as much as I spent sitting at my desk at P.S. 35, where I was in the fifth grade. Of course, I didn't learn penmanship or arithmetic sitting on the stoop, but I watched the people walking up and down the street and I learned from them. And I can even remember sitting on the stoop once, a long time ago, and having an astronomy lesson of sorts.

It was summer, and I was out during the evening with some of the other kids on the block. We were trying to count the stars in the sky. Someone—I think it was Ann's older brother, Paul—told me that there was a star in the sky for every person. It seemed a reasonable idea. There are a lot of people on earth and a lot of stars in the sky.

"How do you know for sure?" I asked him.

"They taught us at church," he said. He knew that I couldn't refute anything he claimed he learned at church.

"Do I have a star?" I asked. After all, maybe Jewish children didn't get heavenly stars. Maybe that was why they often wore little gold ones on a chain around their neck.

"Of course," Paul said. "Everyone has a star. In fact," he added slyly, "your star is going to fall to earth tomorrow night."

"It is? How do you know?" I asked.

"Haven't you ever heard of falling stars?"

"How does it happen?" I wondered, puzzled.

"It gets too crowded up in the sky, and the star falls down to earth to make room for others. I saw the chart of them at church," he insisted. "Your star is going to fall down right on this street tomorrow night."

Instead of worrying that my star would fall, I became very excited. It seemed wonderful to be able to pick up one's very own star and to possess it. During the next day I spent a lot of time searching in our apartment for a small box, just the right size for a star. Eventually I settled on one lined with cotton that seemed perfect for keeping the star safe and protected. In the evening I sat outside on the stoop clutching my little box and waiting.

14

Neither Paul nor any of his friends were about. They had gone off elsewhere to play that evening. The other children outside were involved in a game of tag in the evening's half dark. From time to time I could hear the muted cheers coming from Yankee Stadium, even though it was almost a mile away. Somebody had gotten a home run. I just sat silently, waiting. I didn't want to miss the moment when my star would land, shining, at my feet.

Gradually it grew darker and harder to distinguish the red-brown brick of the houses on the street. The buildings all looked pretty much alike as if they were members of the same large family. Mothers began opening the windows and shouting for their children to come in and get ready for bed. We lived on the ground floor, so my mother didn't have to shout when she opened our window. My little sister, Lyn, stuck her head from the window too. She was already in her pajamas.

"Just a while longer," I begged. I knew it would fall soon.

After a few minutes my father came outside and sat on the stoop beside me. I showed him the box and told him about my star.

"What star?" he asked, laughing.

I explained to him what Paul had taught me.

"He was just teasing you, honey," my father said. "There isn't going to be a star falling on this street tonight."

"Yes, there is. I know he's telling the truth," I insisted. "It's a sin to tell a lie, and he wouldn't want to go to Hell." I had learned all about the horrors of Hell from my friends. "Dad, you don't understand. Paul learned about it at church. There are lots of things we don't know about because we don't go to church," I said.

"And there are many things I *do* know, even if I don't go to church," he answered, sighing.

He lit a cigarette, and the tip glowed in the darkness. He began to tell me about stars: that there are billions of them in the sky and that they are thousands and thousands of miles away. He said if one of them ever did land on our street, it would be so enormous that it would take up more than our whole block and more than the whole Bronx. "Someday soon I'll take you and Lyn to the planetarium in Manhattan so that you can really learn about stars," he said.

I leaned against my father's shoulder and blinked away the tears that were stinging in my eyes. He was very smart. He had gone to college, and he had read more books than anyone I knew. If he said that there wasn't a star for me in the sky, he was probably right.

"Come," my father said, reaching in his pocket and taking out seven cents. "It's a good night for a Mell-o-roll." He put his arm around my shoulder, and we walked up to the corner where Honig's Candy Store sold ice cream. I knew he was trying to distract me.

"Dad," I asked, as I licked my cylinder of ice cream. "Someday could I have a little star on a chain like the ones some of the girl's wear at school?" Both Ann and Patty had silver crosses, which they wore around their necks, but a star was better than a cross.

"We'll see," he said, shrugging his shoulders. It did not seem at all likely.

Anyhow, after that disappointment over the star, I stopped believing everything the children on the street told me. I refused to believe that I was going to Hell when I died just because I didn't go to church every Sunday. And I didn't believe that God was my father because I already had a perfectly good one. He was the only father on our street who had gone to college. If it weren't for the depression, he would have continued studying and he would have become a teacher. But he had to find a job and that was how he started working at the post office. When he came home at night, if he wasn't too tired after supper, he took out his typewriter and put it on the kitchen table. He was writing a novel. He had been working on it for as long as I could remember. Sometimes I could hear him typing when I was falling asleep. It was as if we had a ghost in the kitchen, typing, typing away in the dark.

But I didn't believe in ghosts, and I got angry with Ann when she started telling me about the Holy Ghost. Still, I couldn't help being intrigued by the special rituals that Ann and Patty observed. They crossed themselves whenever we walked past the church, and they both had rosary beads, which they used when they said their prayers. I liked the nuns in their long, black dresses and stiff, white collars. Their faces were so calm. I always wondered what they could be thinking.

Sometimes Ann or Patty invited me to

attend catechism class with them. But even though I was curious, I also felt shy, so I didn't accept their invitations. Besides I think my parents would have objected if I had wanted to go. Just because we didn't do anything to act Jewish didn't mean that they wanted me to start studying to be a Catholic. Yet my life was full of contradictions. On Sundays, my mother insisted that Lyn and I put on our best clothes. "There's no reason to look like ragamuffins, just because you don't go to church," she always said, when we protested. "And besides, you don't want to stick out like a sore thumb." So there we sat on the stoop on Sunday afternoons, Ann and Patty feeling holy and Lyn and I feeling self-conscious. Of course we stuck out like sore thumbs.

Just the way I did now, sitting on the stoop when everyone else was off at school. Lyn was lucky. She had a sore throat and had to stay inside. But I had to remain out in the sunshine, because my mother made a big fuss about getting lots of fresh air. She once started telling me about how during the war a woman in France who was hiding with her baby in an apartment risked being caught every day when she held the infant up to the open window to get a little sunshine. My mother had read about her in the newspaper.

"But why was she hiding?" I asked.

"Never mind that. The important thing is that she wanted fresh air and couldn't get it. You can," my mother answered. She seemed sorry she had mentioned that French woman.

Suddenly I discovered that my index finger was in my mouth. Too late. I had bitten another nail. My parents were always nagging me about that habit, but I couldn't seem to control it. Mostly I didn't notice what I had done until the nail was half bitten, and then there was nothing to do but finish the job. My father even stopped my allowance until I stopped biting my nails. It worked for a couple of weeks, but then school opened, and what with my teacher shouting all the time and the new and harder arithmetic problems, I began all over again. Soon there were only three nails with any white showing on them.

Sometimes in the house, when I was listening to the radio in the evening, my mother would tell me to put on my winter mittens so I wouldn't bite my nails. But you wouldn't catch me wearing mittens outdoors in September! I looked up from my fingers and saw old Mrs. Wallace walking towards me. She was holding the leash of her aged cocker spaniel, Willie. They stopped in front of me.

"How are you today?" Mrs. Wallace asked. To my relief she didn't ask why I wasn't in school.

"I'm OK," I answered politely.

"You're lucky," she said. "You could be blind. Or just imagine you were deaf and

dumb. There are people like that, you know. Be glad you are you."

It was hard not to laugh. I knew that Mrs. Wallace was sincere and meant every word she said. But if you had heard her say the very same words every time you saw her on the street, you would understand how her message had become meaningless. Mrs. Wallace and Willie walked slowly on. I looked down into my lap where I had a book. It was a Nancy Drew mystery that I had borrowed from a girl at school. If I read it slowly, maybe it would last the whole day. That was the trouble with being the best reader in the class. Books never lasted long enough. I envied Nancy Drew. Like the Bobbsey Twins, and all the other people in books, she wasn't Jewish. I couldn't think of a single person in a book who was Jewish like me. Nancy Drew wasn't different or odd the way I was. She was just like everyone else except she solved mysteries.

I figured out a way to sit on one of my hands, the one with two of my three grown nails, and balance the book with my knees. I would read and forget who or where I was. The day would pass, and Yom Kippur would be over. Things could always be worse, as Mrs. Wallace had suggested. Suppose I were blind.

2
Friends and Enemies

I had three jobs about the house: dusting every Saturday morning, drying the dishes after supper every evening, and going out to buy the New York *Times* at Honig's Candy Store every morning, which was a waste of three cents. The *Times* didn't have any funny papers like the *Daily News* or the *Mirror* or the *Herald Tribune*. I never used to look at the newspaper at all. Those days, whenever I glanced at the front page, it was full of news about the war and fighting. Even though the war had been over for more than two years, all the talk on the radio and in the paper was still about it.

When I was little I used to wonder what there would be to say when the war was over. I thought there wouldn't be any news at all and that the announcer would have to speak about the weather very slowly to take up the whole five-minute broadcast. Then I saw that I was wrong. The bad news seemed to go on and on. Whenever I looked at the headlines, I saw that there was a lot written about Jews, too. I guess that was why I thought about my religion more than I did in the past. And, of course, I was older. Worrying is a part of getting older. I knew because my mother was a worrier too.

Every summer she worried about our getting polio. She wouldn't let Lyn or me go to the swimming pool or to the movies during the summer months because she said it might be dangerous. She was always scrubbing things—clothes, dishes, the kitchen floor. She said cleanliness was very important. But Patty Quinn's mother used to say everyone needs to eat a peck of dirt before they die.

Patty Quinn and Ann D'Amato lived in the same house that I did, which is why we were best friends. Their apartments were on the second floor, above me, and so in the evening, when the garbage was collected in the dumbwaiter, we could call messages to one another through the smelly air shaft. "Bring your jacks to school tomorrow," I might remind them.

We walked to school together every day, even though we were all in different classes. Ann was the oldest, and so she was half a year ahead of me at school, in 5B. Patty was the youngest, and she was half a year behind me in 4B. I liked being in the middle in 5A. I seemed closer to each of my friends than they were to each other, even if I didn't have the same religion that they did and sometimes felt excluded from that part of their lives. Sometimes Mrs. Quinn said, "Two's company, three's a crowd," when we had a quarrel. My sister, Lyn, was in the second grade, and she tagged along with us too. I always thought *four* was a crowd when Lyn was around!

My mother always wanted Lyn and me to get lots of sunshine because it had vitamins. So once or twice a week, when the weather was good, she took us to the park on the Grand Concourse, which was about six blocks away. There wasn't any more sun there than on our street, but because there were some trees and grass and wooden benches for sitting on, she felt it was a healthy place for playing. There were no swings or slides or monkey bars at the park, so once there we had to make up our own games. It wasn't much fun playing with Lyn. She jumped rope and played ball no better than a baby. Of course, there were other kids at the park. I recognized some of them from school.

Sometimes I saw Lois Weiss, Sheila Shapiro, and Marsha Schwartz. I used to stand nearby waiting for one of them to notice me and ask me to play. You would never guess that we had been in the same class together since kindergarten. They acted as if they had never seen me before.

Once they were all jumping rope, and I got up my nerve and asked, "Could I take an end?"

"Sure," said Lois. I was surprised to find her so agreeable, and I started turning the rope together with Sheila while Lois and Marsha took turns jumping. They said the same rhymes that Ann and Patty and I always chanted:

"Strawberry shortcake, cream on top,
Spell me the name of your sweetheart."
and
"Baby in the highchair
Who put her in?
Ma, Pa, Woop-sa-la . . ."

Marsha missed and took an end. Then Lois missed. I handed her my end of the rope. "You said you wanted to take an end," she said. She took the piece of rope from Marsha

31

and left me still holding onto my end. Neither Sheila nor Marsha said anything. I thought Lois was kidding or testing me. But I spent the whole afternoon turning the rope, and I never did any jumping at all. Afterward I thought, Boy, was I stupid! I should have just dropped the rope and walked away. Who wanted to play with Lois Weiss anyhow? Her second teeth were all growing in crooked, and she had eczema on both her arms. Why would anyone want to be her friend?

But for some reason, I did. I was fascinated by Lois and Sheila and Marsha, and I had been secretly watching them for years, ever since I realized that they were Jewish. I thought I could learn more about my religion if they were my friends. They could tell me what they did on the holidays when they stayed home from school. They could explain some of the traditions that I had only vaguely heard about but didn't really understand. How else would I ever learn?

I didn't know why they didn't like me. Or rather, there were several reasons, and I didn't know which was the real one. I was smarter than they were. I knew my grades bothered Lois. She always found an excuse to walk past my desk to see the mark on my arithmetic and spelling papers. Since I usually got 100, I left the paper out for her to see.

Their families were richer than mine. All three girls went to Florida in the winter and to camp in the summer. They had more clothes than I did and housekeepers who walked in the rain to bring their lunches and boots to school when they forgot and left them at home. But if I wasn't jealous of them, why should that matter? At least, I didn't think I was jealous.

I once read in a book about people living on the wrong side of the tracks. There were some old, unused trolley tracks set in the cobblestones on Morris Avenue. My street was on one side of those tracks, and the kids on the

Grand Concourse lived on the other. Perhaps I lived on the wrong side of the tracks. That was a silly reason to dislike someone.

I supposed that Sheila and Marsha and Lois were friends because they lived near each other, just as Ann and Patty and I were best friends for that reason. Sometimes, when I secretly watched Lois Weiss, who was pretending not to know me, I thought, someday I want to be very famous. Then Lois would brag to everyone that she went to school with Geraldine Flam when she was young. And when people came and asked me if I remembered Lois Weiss, I would say, "Lois Weiss? I never heard of her." Or else I would say, "Lois Weiss? Yes, she was the girl who sat next to me in fourth grade and used to copy all the time."

When you were really famous, streets and schools and parks were named after you. Our park had a name: Joyce Kilmer. My mother explained that it was the name of a poet. "Did

she live in the Bronx when she was a girl?"
I asked. To my surprise, not only did Joyce
Kilmer never live in the Bronx, he was a
man!

Most days when we went to the park, Ann
and Patty came along with us. For some reason, no other mother on our block ever went
there. It was another of the little things that
made me different from the other kids on the
street. Sometimes we brought our roller skates.
We liked to skate past the large and elaborate
stone fountain in the center of the park. It had
stone fish and mermaids with naked breasts,
and during the summer water splashed out of
spigots set in the stone. Some children took
off their shoes and waded in the water when
the weather was hot. But my mother once saw
a dog peeing in the fountain, and so Lyn and
I had been forbidden to stick even a finger
into the water. Luckily, there was a different
fountain where you could get a drink, and
dogs couldn't reach that one.

On Yom Kippur my mother had worried that Lyn might be getting whooping cough. It turned out to be only a bad cold. The first sunny day after Lyn was well again, my mother announced that we would go to the park after school. As usual, Ann and Patty came along with us. As soon as we got there, I suggested that we run to the fountain for a drink.

I started running without even waiting to see if the others were following me. In another week the water would be turned off until the spring.

"What shall we do now?" asked Patty, when she caught up with me at the fountain.

"Do you have any chalk? We could make a potsy."

She felt the pocket of her dress. "I forgot to bring some," she said.

"Maybe we can find a piece on the ground," I suggested hopefully. "Somebody might have dropped a piece." We started looking on the sidewalk, and when Ann and Lyn caught up with us, they looked too.

I didn't find any chalk, but suddenly, before me on the ground, I spotted a stick of gum in its wrapper. I picked it up and considered chewing it. Someone must have lost it. On the other hand, it might be poison gum that someone had left to trick us.

"Where did you get that?" asked Lyn, seeing the gum in my hand. "I want a piece too!" Everything was her business. She made me angry.

I thought for a second, and then I said, "Here. You can have it."

Lyn grabbed the gum and didn't even bother to say thanks. She unwrapped it and stuffed it quickly into her mouth. She was afraid that I would change my mind.

"How come you didn't give me any?" asked Patty. "I would have shared with you."

"You'll see," I said in a whisper.

"What?"

"Wait and see. This may be the end of Lynda Flam."

"What are you talking about?" Ann and Patty both asked, as Lyn skipped ahead of us.

"I think that gum may be poisoned. Then I'll be rid of her forever."

"You're crazy," said Ann. "Where did you buy poisoned gum around here? They don't sell it at Honig's!"

"I didn't buy it," I explained. "I found it on the ground when I was looking for a piece of chalk."

"You did? You found a piece of poisoned gum right here in the park? Why did you give it to Lyn? That wasn't very nice. If she dies, you'll go straight to Hell," said Patty. It wasn't the first time she had threatened me. Both Ann and Patty often spoke with a tone of superiority. They knew things I didn't, and God was on their side, not mine.

"Jewish people don't go to Hell. Only Catholic people," I answered. I wasn't certain, but

38

my answer did quiet them both for a moment.

"Do you think she will die slowly or fast?" asked Ann with fascination.

"When you touch the third rail, you die instantly," said Patty. Her father worked at the railroad yards, and she was always talking about the third rail.

"Maybe she won't die at all," I said. "This is only practice. I'm not even sure that this piece of gum is poisoned."

"Oh," said Ann disappointedly. "I thought it was going to be like when Patty told Lorraine to put beads in her ears." Lorraine was Patty's sister, and she was four years old. They had to take her to the hospital to get the beads out.

"Well, if Lyn does die, you'll go to jail," said Patty. "Even Jewish people go there."

I hadn't thought about that possibility. I was too busy thinking about having the bedroom all to myself and not having to share everything, including my friends, with Lyn.

I looked at Lyn. She had stopped skipping and had gone to pet a little puppy on a leash. I suddenly remembered how much fun we had giggling in our beds at night. In the darkness we were always good friends. I didn't really want to kill her. I just needed a vacation from being her sister for a few days.

Lyn looked up at me and smiled. "Don't you wish we had a dog?" she said.

"How do you feel?" asked Patty.

"OK," said Lyn.

"How's the gum?" Ann asked her.

"I spit it out."

"Why?" we all asked at the same time.

"It burned my tongue."

For a moment I wondered if that was an effect of the poison. But then Lyn said, "I like fruit gum best, and it was cinnamon."

We all took turns petting the puppy and then played follow-the-leader, climbing on benches and running around the trees. There were lots of signs that said *Keep Off the Grass*, but we never paid any attention to them. When we passed the bench where my mother was sitting, she called to us.

"Time to go home now," she said. She was sitting and talking with another mother, whom she knew from the Parents' Association. (My mother had been Secretary and Treasurer and Vice-President of the Parents' Association over the years and went to lots of committee meeetings that made plans for improving P.S. 35.)

"Already? We just got here," I protested.

"I want to stop at the vegetable store on the way home," she said. "Here," she offered, opening her pocketbook. "Does anyone want a piece of gum?" She didn't really approve of the stuff, but she thought it would keep my mouth too busy for nail-biting.

We all accepted. A minute later, Lyn spit hers out. "It's peppermint," she said.

3
Piano Lessons

It's funny how one thing can lead to another. When Ann's mother was a little girl, she wanted to play the piano, but she never was given the opportunity. Then one day a new family moved to our street. The moving men took all day to get their piano into the apartment, because they couldn't fit it up the staircase. They had to haul it up the outside of the building with ropes lowered from the roof. We all stood about, watching and cheering. It was more exciting than the noisy coal deliveries or even the annual sewer cleaning, when a man in a dirty outfit took all the muck out of the sewer at the foot of our block. There usually were about a dozen Spaldeen balls that were retrieved in the process, so black that I could never believe that once they were bright pink.

When Mrs. D'Amato discovered that Mrs. Wulf, the owner of the piano, gave lessons, she decided that Ann should study with her. Ann began bragging to me about how she was going to become a famous concert pianist, and I began thinking about how wonderful it would be to take lessons too. So I started nagging my mother, and even though she had never wanted piano lessons as a child, my mother decided that I should study some music also. In this way, Mrs. Wulf got two new students the first week in October.

Our mothers devised a plan. As neither the D'Amato family nor we owned a piano, the only chance Ann and I would have to play the instrument would be during our lesson time. So they arranged with Mrs. Wulf that we would take our lessons together. Instead of each of us having a private hour every week, we would go as a team. Ann would have fifteen minutes of lesson time, and then it would be my turn, then fifteen minutes more for Ann, and fifteen minutes more for me. If we went twice a week, we would each be exposed to two hours of piano lessons, which would at least partially compensate for the lack of practicing generally expected of piano students.

I don't know who was more nervous when we went to our first lesson, Ann or me. I looked at the nails on both my hands. I wondered if Mrs. Wulf would comment on their bitten condition and I worried that it would impair my ability at the piano. I wondered too if we would see Mrs. Wulf's son. I had glimpsed him on the street a couple of times, but I never saw him at school. Ann rang the doorbell. After a minute Mrs. Wulf opened the door. "Come in, ladies," she said, smiling at us. Her accent was pronounced and sounded very strange to us. She had come to America from Germany just before the war, and although she could speak English, she did not sound like our teachers or parents. When she smiled, we could see that one of her front teeth was made of gold.

"She must be very rich. I guess she makes lots of money from giving lessons," Ann had told me.

We walked through the hallway of the apartment. It smelled different from our apartments. There was something sweet in the air, and it tickled my nose. I began to worry that I might start sneezing. Luckily, I had remembered to put a clean handkerchief in my dress pocket that morning.

We were led into a room that held nothing but a piano and a stool and two chairs. One chair was next to the piano, and the second was a little way off.

"Who is to go first?" asked Mrs. Wulf, after

she had pocketed the two dollar bills that we handed her. The lessons were to cost a dollar a week.

"You go," we each said, pointing to the other.

"We will start with Ann," said Mrs. Wulf. I noticed that each *W* came out with the sound of a *V*. So as Ann sat down on the piano stool, I repeated to myself, "Ve vill start vith Ann." The sound made me want to laugh.

Mrs. Wulf showed us where middle C was on the piano. It would be easy to remember because just underneath it was a keyhole. I wondered if she locked up her piano every night before she went to bed. She had explained that the keys were made of ivory. I also wondered how many elephant tusks were needed to make the keys for a single piano.

"You girls will have to work hard," said Mrs. Wulf. "You must concentrate even when it is not your turn," she said, looking right at me. How did she know I was thinking about the big, grey elephants in the Bronx Zoo? "Do you know that when Mozart was your age, he had already composed many sonatas for the clavichord and the violin?"

I wondered if Mozart was another of Mrs. Wulf's students. And what was a sonata or a clavichord? I was embarrassed that this Mozart kid had done so much by the time he was ten years old. I looked at Ann. For once I was glad that she was older. Today we were both the same age, but in a few weeks she would be having her birthday and be ahead of me again. Imagine! Soon Ann would be eleven, and she still wouldn't have composed any sonatas! At least, I had a little more time to try. And besides, I thought proudly, I had already written some poems. One poem, which was about Abraham Lincoln, had even been printed in the Parents' Association *Bulletin*. Ann hadn't written any poems at all.

Mrs. Wulf looked at the little watch that she wore pinned to her dress. "Now it is your turn," she said to me. Ann and I exchanged seats.

"Where is middle C?" Mrs. Wulf asked. I looked at the keyhole and promptly hit the correct note with my finger.

"Good," said Mrs. Wulf. "Now show me the C above middle C."

I looked at Mrs. Wulf. Then I looked down at the piano. There were no more keyholes. How could I ever find another C note? Piano lessons were going to be harder than I had thought.

Before I had a chance to say that I didn't know, a phone rang in another room of the apartment.

"Oh, excuse me," said Mrs. Wulf. And she hurried off to answer it.

I turned to Ann. "Show me another C before she comes back."

Ann was looking pale and frightened.

"Gerry," she said, "I think we should get out of here."

"Why? Don't you know where the C notes are either?" I asked.

"No," said Ann. "Look at that." She pointed to a heavy volume on the top of the piano. The lettering on the spine read *Chopin*. "It's a book about chopping people up. I think we should escape while we can."

Everyone always said that Ann had a morbid imagination. The thought of Mrs. Wulf chopping us up seemed very unlikely to me. Still, there was no denying what was printed on the book.

"It's spelled wrong," I said. "It should have a *G* at the end."

"It's probably the German way of spelling it," reasoned Ann.

"Watch if she's coming, and I'll look inside the book," I whispered. I reached up and lifted down the heavy volume.

I opened it with shaking hands. Would there be colored pictures of bleeding children inside? "It's only music," I said, showing Ann. I was almost disappointed. Discovering that our piano teacher was really a murderer in disguise would have been exciting, like Nancy Drew solving a crime or like the adventure programs we used to listen to on the radio when we were younger: *Tom Mix* or *Captain Midnight*.

"It might be a secret code," said Ann. She was not yet ready to give up her suspicions. "After all, she is *German* and you know that the Germans did some terrible things in the war."

I nodded my head. "We'll have to keep watching her," I said. I heard Mrs. Wulf's steps in the hallway, and I quickly replaced the book on top of the piano.

"Quick," I begged Ann. "Show me the C above middle C."

4
A Rainy Day

Ann D'Amato liked to make plans. After her sister Rita got married last spring, Ann started making plans for her own wedding. Even though she wasn't eleven yet, she liked to think ahead. She also liked to plan for others. So she was planning that I would marry her brother, Paul. That way we could be sisters, she said.

Of course, there were still a few things to work out. In the first place, Ann said I would have to convert to Catholicism. In the second place, Paul didn't particularly like me. I thought he was OK. He was tall and had dark hair and dark eyes. But I had always imagined that the man I would marry would look more like Alan Ladd or Cornell Wilde, whose faces I saw when I licked off the lids from a Dixie cup of ice cream.

Paul kidded around a lot, and he wasn't very good at school. Last year he was almost left back, but my mother went with Mrs. D'Amato and spoke to the principal and persuaded him that Paul would study hard during the summer. And then my mother was the one who checked his arithmetic problems and reminded Mrs. D'Amato that he should spend half an hour reading each evening.

Sometimes, if Ann and I were arguing about something, she threatened that Paulie wouldn't marry me. "He'll marry Patty instead," she said, hoping to make me jealous.

"Maybe Paulie doesn't like her," I would answer back. But all the while I was thinking, Maybe Paulie doesn't want to marry me.

Even though Ann and Patty and I were best friends, we had disagreements and fights. Sometimes I thought they were caused by our parents and not by us at all. For example, whenever it rained and we couldn't go outside to play, my mother would let me have *one* friend in to play. Our apartment was too small for me to be permitted to invite both girls at the same time. If I invited Ann, then Patty was hurt. And, of course, if I invited Patty, then Ann got mad. And it was even worse if Ann invited Patty and not me to play at her house. So I hated rainy Saturdays because I had to worry about where I was going to play and with whom.

I loved to go to Patty's apartment. Her mother was constantly baking fresh cookies or pies. Mrs. Quinn always said funny things, too. Once she heard me sneezing, and she said, "One a wish, two a kiss, three a letter, four something better." I sneezed four times. But then I sneezed several times more. It wasn't better; it was worse. I was getting a cold.

And another time when I was at Patty's, she dropped a spoon and Mrs. Quinn said it meant that a woman would come to visit. Sure enough, about ten minutes later, the doorbell rang and it was Mrs. Vice, from upstairs, who came to borrow an egg and stayed for a cup of tea.

At Ann's apartment things were different. First of all, Mrs. D'Amato almost always had a huge pot of tomato sauce simmering on the stove. The spicy smell filled the entire apartment. The D'Amato apartment always looked as if the family were getting ready to move. There were piles of clutter on the floor and in the hallway, and on the chairs in the living room there were often mounds of laundry that was waiting to be ironed.

Whenever Lyn and I didn't put our things away and our room was a mess, my mother grumbled under her breath, "This place is getting to look like the D'Amatos'." But even though she wasn't a good housekeeper, everyone liked Mrs. D'Amato. I always pretended that everything was in order at their home, and I sat right on top of the laundry on the chairs, just as if it wasn't there.

The Saturday after Ann and I started taking our piano lessons, it rained. I had just finished my weekly dusting chore when the doorbell rang. It was Ann, inviting me upstairs to play with her. I was relieved not to have to make any choices. Now if Patty got angry, I could just say, "I couldn't help it. Ann invited me to her house."

"It's not fair!" Lyn started pouting. "I want to go too!" She must have said those words a hundred times a day.

"What shall we do?" Ann asked, when we were upstairs sitting on her unmade bed.

"Did you practice for the next lesson yet?" I asked. We had figured out a method of pretending to play the piano. We would look at the exercises that Mrs. Wulf had given us, and while we sat at the kitchen table we would move our fingers up and down as if we were playing the instrument. It was a very quiet way to play the piano, and I didn't have to start exactly at middle C.

"Yes," said Ann. "Did you?"

"Yes," I said. "I've been trying to think what we should do to become famous like Mozart. I don't think we'll ever be good enough to compose music. So maybe we should invent something."

"Like what?" asked Ann.

"Maybe we could invent a new machine that does something just by pushing a button. That would make us famous."

"What kind of machine?"

"Maybe a machine that"—I paused to think of something really clever—"a machine that answers the telephone for you," I said.

"How about a machine that does your

homework for you?" suggested Ann. Her family didn't have a telephone, but Ann did get a lot of homework.

"Or a machine that washes and dries the dishes for you?"

"Or a machine that cleans the house for you?" said Ann.

"That's already been invented," I reminded her. "It's a Hoover. We have one. Didn't you ever see it?"

"I forgot," said Ann.

"Maybe we could invent a new food," I suggested.

"Like strawberry potato cheese sauce."

"Ugh!" I shrieked. "How about mashed hamburgers with chocolate carrot syrup."

For a long time we amused each other with our foods. Then Ann got an idea. "We could invent a new perfume," she said. She showed me a box filled with perfumes and toilet water that had belonged to her sister, Rita. "I don't think she needs these any more now that she's married. We could mix them together and invent a new perfume."

"That's a great idea," I agreed. "But would we become famous?"

"Sure. Lots of women would want to wear it. We would become rich too."

Ann went into the kitchen and asked her mother if she had an empty bottle that we could play with. Mrs. D'Amato found a small jar with two olives left in it. Ann and I each ate one of the olives, and then we rinsed out the jar. We mixed Parisian Evening and Summer Nights and Hidden Mysteries all together. Then we poured in some Gladiola, too.

The sweet smells began to tickle my nose, and I sneezed twice. Once a wish, twice a kiss, I remembered. But Paulie was not at home.

"We'll give this a fancy name," said Ann.

"Let's call it Heart's Delight," I said.

"Ah, Heart's Delight. That's perfect," said Ann admiringly. She put the top onto the olive jar and shook the contents together. When she opened it, some of the liquid dripped down the sides of the jar. We wiped it up with the sleeves of our blouses. It made us smell wonderful. Then I sneezed four times in succession. Three a letter, four something better, I remembered. Better than a letter or better than Paulie, I wondered fleetingly.

"We will become famous at last," said Ann. "This was a good plan."

"I'll write an advertisement for it," I offered. "Maybe they'll sing it on the radio for us." I thought for a minute:

> "Wear Heart's Delight
> Every night
> Then you will smell
> Just swell."

"How do you do it just like that?" asked Ann. "You didn't even have to write it down.

You're a real poet," she said. "You'll probably be famous for your poetry, too, when you grow up."

"Do you really think so?" I asked. She had expressed one of my secret dreams.

"Sure," said Ann, dabbing some of the perfume onto her wrists and earlobes. "Look how fast you made up the advertisement. Maybe Mrs. Wulf can help us set it to music."

Mrs. D'Amato came into the room to offer us some lunch. The perfume made her sneeze, too, but I forgot to count the number of times. During lunch, which was fat shells stuffed with cheese and covered with tomato sauce, I thought of something. "Do you remember the formula?" I asked Ann.

"What formula? That's what babies drink."

"The ingredients to make Heart's Delight. Do you remember how much we used of each perfume?"

"It doesn't matter," Ann reassured me.

"We'll just mix them any which way, and no one will know the difference."

It will be wonderful to be famous, I thought. Just like Mozart and Joyce Kilmer.

After lunch it was still raining. I went downstairs and begged my mother to let me go to the movies with Ann. It cost twelve cents. She agreed on condition that we take Lyn along with us and that I dress warmly. We rang Patty's doorbell, and she came along with us too. They were showing a picture with lots of singing and dancing, which was the kind of movie we all liked best, and it had the perfect name to distract us on a rainy day. It was called *Blue Skies*.

5
Edgar

One Thursday, early in December, I had to go to my piano lesson alone. Ann was in bed with a sore throat. I felt shy as I rang Mrs. Wulf's doorbell. It was much more comfortable to go to lessons together with Ann, even if we had both decided that our piano teacher wasn't a murderer.

Mrs. Wulf seemed pleased to have me by myself. "Now I will get to know you a little bit better," she said. "First the lesson, and then we will have a cup of tea."

I didn't like the taste of tea, and all during my scales I made more mistakes than usual because I was thinking of reasons why I had to go home.

"No, you must stay at least for a few minutes," said Mrs. Wulf at the end of the half hour, when I said that I must go home. "After all, you usually remain a full hour, so your mother won't be expecting you yet." So, helplessly, I followed Mrs. Wulf into the living room of the apartment.

"Now you wait here, and I'll call Edgar," she said.

Edgar was her son. He was about the same age as Paul D'Amato, but I had never seen him join the other boys on the street in a game of stickball or ring-a-levio. Edgar was serious-looking, and whenever I saw him he was carrying a briefcase full of school books.

"How do you do?" said Edgar, holding out his hand to me. I had seen grown-ups greet one another that way, but kids never did. Edgar looked so silly with his hand stretched out that I had to smother a giggle. I shook his hand. "Hi," I said.

"I'm in 8A," he said. He had a German accent like his mother, but it was less notice-able. "What grade are you in?"

"I'm in 5A," I told him.

"Even though we have moved and I've changed schools several times, I was skipped a grade," said Edgar. "So actually, I'm only two years older than you." He spoke in a nice way, not boasting at all, just trying to show me that he was really closer to my age than I would have thought.

Mrs. Wulf joined us, carrying a tray with a teapot and cups and also a plate of cookies. To my relief, she asked if I would rather have a glass of milk. The cookies were in two pieces with a filling of jam in the middle. They were delicious, and I was suddenly glad that I had been asked to stay. I wondered if Mrs. Wulf would invite me another time together with Ann.

But then she said, "There are not many Jewish children in this neighborhood. Edgar hasn't made any friends here yet."

1

From the way she spoke, I realized that I had been singled out for this special treat because Edgar and his mother were Jewish and so was I. It's true that the only other Jewish family on our street were the Honigs, who owned the candy store. But as I wasn't very Jewish, I felt that I didn't deserve the cookie that I was chewing on.

"Edgar could make friends with the children on the street, the way I do," I suggested. "They're very nice."

"Yes, but they are not the same," said Mrs. Wulf. "Besides," she went on, almost as if he wasn't sitting right there, "Edgar is a very serious boy with serious interests, and they are always playing wild games."

"I have a stamp collection," said Edgar. "Would you like to see it?"

I nodded my head. Edgar went to his room and returned carrying a heavy album filled with postage stamps.

"I have some stamps too," I told him. "You know, my father works at the post office, and he brings me stamps that get torn off packages or from letters in the dead-letter file. But my collection is really a mess. Yours is very neat," I added with admiration.

"Perhaps we could trade stamps with one another," Edgar offered. "Why don't you bring your stamps here, and we'll look at them together? I can help you."

So that is how it happened that the very next day, which was Friday and not the day for my piano lesson, I returned to Mrs. Wulf's apartment with a large brown envelope filled with stamps and a small album that was practically empty. Edgar looked at the confusion of stamps. "Leave these with me. I'll help you sort them out," he said. "Look, here are duplicates already." He pulled a handful of stamps from the envelope and showed them to me.

Then he showed me a map of the world that was on the wall of his room, and he pointed out the little black dot that represented Berlin, the city where he was born.

"Were you sad to move away from there?" I asked.

"I have only a few memories from when I was very young," he said. "We didn't leave until 1939, and we were very fortunate to get out. Many of my relatives did not."

"Why did you leave?" I asked.

"That is a silly question," said Edgar. "We had to leave because we are Jewish." He paused a minute, and then he said, "If we had stayed we would have been killed."

My parents rarely spoke about what happened during the war, but I had picked up little bits from news broadcasts on the radio and from overhearing things my classmates said.

"You didn't have to tell people that you

were Jewish," I said. "If you didn't tell them, they wouldn't know. Lots of people don't know that I'm Jewish."

"It sounds very simple to you," said Edgar, "but the Germans had records of all the people. Even people who had converted to Christianity were murdered when it was discovered that they had Jewish parents or grandparents."

I shuddered at his words. "But why?" I asked. I couldn't understand.

"Because they hated the Jews," said Edgar.

"That is awful," I said. "I'm glad we aren't Jewish anymore."

"But you *are* Jewish. You just said so."

"Well, we used to be. But now we don't really have any religion at all. I'm an American and nothing else," I said.

"That wouldn't have stopped the Nazis if they had gotten here."

The war was not so long ago. I could still

remember the blackout drills at night and the air-raid drills at school when we hid under our desks in preparation for an attack by the Germans or the Japanese. We used to wear identification tags around our necks, too. First they gave us cardboard ones, but when the war continued, they gave us stronger ones made of heavy plastic. The teacher said they were necessary in case families became separated or if we were wounded during a bombing. Afterward I used to lie awake in bed at night terrified whenever I heard airplanes flying overhead. I still shivered sometimes at night when I heard airplanes, even though the war was over forever.

"Things will be different now that Palestine has been recognized as a Jewish state," said Edgar. "Imagine a Jewish homeland after so many centuries!"

"What do you mean—a Jewish homeland?" I asked.

"A place for all Jews to live. So we never again have to fear anti-Semitism. Our own country!" he said. His voice rose with excitement.

"That sounds awful," I said. "Why can't people live wherever they want? All my friends are Roman Catholic, and they don't have to live in Rome. Why should Jews have to live all together in one place?"

"Maybe because they haven't had their own place for two thousand years," said Edgar. "We wanted to go to Palestine, but we couldn't get papers. Then my aunt and uncle managed to get papers for us to come to America, just in time. But someday I want to go to Palestine to live. That's why I'm studying Hebrew." He smiled at me. "Would you like to come to my Bar Mitzvah next fall?" he asked.

"What's that?" I asked, though I remembered vaguely hearing some of the kids talking about Bar Mitzvahs at school.

"Don't you know anything?" asked Edgar. "That's the religious ceremony when a Jewish boy becomes thirteen years old. After I become a Bar Mitzvah, I'll be able to participate in the services at the synagogue."

"I've never been to a synagogue," I admitted. There was no point in pretending to know all these things that Edgar was talking about. He would see through me very quickly.

"Never?" Edgar gasped. "What kind of a Jew are you?"

"I guess I'm not really a Jew at all," I said, getting up to leave. "I'm only one thing. I'm an American."

"Wait," said Edgar. "Will you do me a favor and read something?" He handed me a Manila envelope. "It's a composition that I had to write for school. I think you should read it. I got an A plus on it, and my teacher isn't even Jewish."

"What's that got to do with anything?" I

asked, as I slid the handwritten sheets out of the envelope. I tried to imagine Ann or Patty asking me to read one of their school compositions when I went to their homes. It was not exactly polite to brag about your A's or make your friends read your reports. But the title hit my eye instantly: *Why I Am Proud to Be a Jew*.

"The subject was to write about something that makes you proud," explained Edgar. "Most of the boys wrote about hitting a home run in a stickball game or something like that. The only other A in the class was a girl who wrote about being proud of her uncle, who was killed in the war."

I started reading. For someone who was still learning English, Edgar used a lot of big words. His main point seemed to be that even though the fact that he was Jewish meant that he had to flee from Germany, still he was proud of his heritage. One phrase was repeated several times, "responsibility to history."

I read the composition through two times. Then I asked Edgar for a piece of paper. This is what I copied:

Now that I am in a new land with new traditions and customs, it would be simple enough to adopt all the new ways and forget the past of my ancestors. But I feel I have a responsibility to history and to all those relatives before me who have held so firmly to their beliefs. Jews have a history of morality, compassion, and courage. I am proud and not afraid to assume the responsibility that my heritage brings. I am proud to be a Jew.

These were words I wanted to think about. And I knew Edgar was very pleased that I wrote out what he had to say.

6
The Swastika

When I went home and was helping my mother set the table for supper, I asked her why the Germans hated the Jews so much. She shrugged her shoulders. "They were sick in the head," she said.

Before I could ask anything more, Lyn came into the room. She had a way of appearing when I didn't want her around. And her sharp ears had already picked up a phrase. "Who is sick in the head?" she asked, looking eagerly from my mother to me.

"Nobody," said my mother. "Nothing was said to concern you." And so we started to talk about other things. The whole subject would have been dropped right there, as usual, except for a peculiar coincidence that very evening. We had macaroni and cheese for dinner, and my mother used up all the milk. She handed me a quarter and the empty bottle to return and sent me around the corner to pick up another quart. When I came back to our building, my father was standing in the outer hallway. He didn't notice me at first because he was busy drawing something on the mailbox. "What are you doing?" I asked, but even as I said the words, I guessed what occupied him.

For as long as I could remember there had been a swastika scratched onto the brass grill of the mailboxes in the front hallway. When I was very little I thought it was a strange way of making the number four. But when I became older, I learned that it was the symbol of the Nazis. Sometimes I saw swastikas drawn in chalk on the street, but they were always washed away by the rain. The one on the mailbox was scratched too deep, and it would always remain. But someone kept drawing over the lines, using them as the basis for a cartoon. Sometimes the lines of the swastika formed a motor car with wheels and a hood drawn in black pencil. Then Mr. O'Connell, our super, would clean the building, washing the halls and polishing the brass mailboxes, and the swastika returned again after the pencil marks were cleaned away. But a day or two later there would be a new drawing. Perhaps a fat dancing lady wearing high-heeled shoes. I never knew who the artist was until now. It was my father.

"Since I can't undo the art work that is here, I like to change it," my father said with sarcasm."

"What difference does it make?" I asked. "It gets washed off all the time."

"The swastika is a sign of hate. There is no real reason to leave it here to find allies," he said.

"I don't understand."

"There are a lot of people in the world who hate Jews. The Nazi symbol reminds them.

Even on this street, there are people who feel this way. These lines," he said, pointing to the scratches on the mailbox, "were made a week after we moved into this building."

"But why do people hate Jews?" I asked. "We didn't do anything bad."

"Hate grows out of ignorance and fear," he answered. "Jews are different in their traditions and customs, and people don't understand them and become afraid of them. I don't particularly believe in all those old traditions and customs. But still, I'm considered a Jew and some people dislike me because of it."

"Were any of your relatives killed by the Nazis?" I asked.

"Who knows? There may have been some distant Pflaumenbaum cousins still in Germany when the war began," my father said. "But I don't know of any personally. Just some cousins on the West Coast."

"Do you think we have a responsibility to history?" I asked, remembering the words I had copied from Edgar's composition. "Don't you think if we are Jews it is our responsibility to act as Jews and worry about other Jews, even if they aren't related to us?"

"It is merely chance that I was born a Jew and you were born a Jew. We can't control chance, but we can try," my father said, shrugging his shoulders. "Therefore, I pray or don't pray as I wish. You mustn't get upset when you hear people talking about the Nazis. The Nazi rule was a terrible period in history, but it is over. In ten years, no one will remember what the Nazis did. Who remembers the massacre of the Armenians during the First World War? It's impossible to live with such memories. So, in time, even the Jews will forget. And we were very fortunate not to be in Europe. We're lucky to live here, even if every once in a while someone does something like draw a swastika on the mailbox," he said, pointing again to the scratches. "We're safe here. We can be ourselves. And we don't have to act like Jews just because of the chance of birth."

"Ann and Patty say that God plans everything," I protested. "They say there is a reason for everything that happens. So there must be a reason we are Jews and not Christians."

"Yes," my father agreed reluctantly. "People who believe in God always say he has a grand plan for the universe. But I don't believe there is a God."

For the second time that day I thought about the nights during the war when I had shivered under my covers because I heard airplanes droning overhead. Always during those nights I had whispered into the darkness to God, asking him to protect me and my family. Perhaps I did so because I had heard Ann and Patty talking about him so much. I didn't know why exactly, but I did feel he existed.

"There is a God!" I said. "I'm sure of it!" And as if to punctuate my words, the bottle of milk that I had been holding slid out of its paper bag and crashed onto the tile floor of the hallway. My oxfords were spattered with milk, and there was broken glass all around us.

"Do you think that was God's plan or was it chance?" asked my father, stepping out of the puddle of milk he was standing in.

"Here," he said, handing me some money, "go buy another bottle of milk before the delicatessen closes, and I'll take care of this mess. You'd better hurry. It's almost time to listen to 'Baby Snooks'," In our family that was one radio program we all liked, and we always listened together.

As I walked back up the street toward the

store, I couldn't help feeling as if my head were also filled with slivers of broken glass and cold, wet milk sloshing about inside it. There were too many thoughts within me that didn't fit together. If only I could make Edgar's words and my father's cook until they blended and made more sense. If only one's thoughts could jell like a smooth pudding or custard, that would have been perfect.

7
A Sore Thumb

Christmas came and passed. Who could I tell
that Christmas embarrassed me? I couldn't
tell my parents, both of whom spent the
weeks before the holiday shopping and planning wonderful surprises for Lyn and me.
"You are so lucky," my mother said, as we
decorated the tree, which we had every year.
When I smelled the fragrance of the pine and
when I ate the spicy pfeffernuesse cookies
that my father brought home from a special
German bakery near the post office, I wanted
to agree. But I couldn't explain to my mother
why I lied to Edgar Wulf and told him that
we were having lots of company during the
vacation week, so he couldn't come to my
house. I didn't want him to see the Christmas

tree. He wouldn't have been able to understand why it was there. Jewish people are not supposed to have Christmas trees.

"It isn't just a religious holiday. It's become an American tradition, a holiday for everyone. Why do you suppose the post office is closed on Christmas?" my father said, when I hinted at my discomfort at our celebrating the holiday.

"I always wanted a tree when I was a child," he said. Of course, he pointed with amusement to the six-pointed star on the top of our tree. It was his little joke. Christians always had a five-pointed star. The star with six points was called the Star of David, and that was a Jewish symbol. He seemed to think that the sixth point on the star made our tree kosher.

So Lyn and I hung up stockings, just like Ann and Patty and the other children on our street. And we also got packages with new games. Why should it have embarrassed me to be so lucky? I didn't understand myself.

This business of the holidays was just one of a hundred things I wanted to discuss with my mother and father. But it was impossible to talk about most things. Lyn was always about with that special little-sister sense. If I wanted a private conversation, she was sure to appear. I never realized how little time alone I had with either of my parents without her interrupting and confusing the issues. Then I got a sore thumb, and I had a whole day for talking.

This was how it happened: I had noticed that the cuticle around my thumb was red and tender, but it hadn't really bothered me at all. Then I woke in the middle of one night with a start. I had been dreaming that I was petting Mrs. Wallace's old dog, Willie. Suddenly the dog turned and bit my thumb. I woke with a dreadful throbbing in my finger and thought how strange dreams can be. Willie was so old that she didn't have any teeth. How could she possibly bite someone? And then I realized that although I had been dreaming and I was now awake, my left thumb was still aching. It felt as though a small heart were beating inside it.

I lay in bed wondering if I should wake my parents. Perhaps the pain would go away if I thought about something else. I breathed slowly and deeply and thought about my next birthday. I wondered if I had caught a rare disease that started with the fingers and then spread to the rest of the body. Possibly I would never have an eleventh birthday.

I began to pray. I didn't pray like Ann and Patty with special words that I had memorized. Instead, I made up my own words as if I were talking. Once Patty asked me if I was a Communist. "What an awful thing to say!" I said with a gasp. "I thought you were my friend, Patty Quinn. I'm just as good an American as you are!"

"Well, they told us at church that Communists don't believe in God," Patty had said. "And you don't ever go anywhere to pray."

But the fact was that I often said little prayers in my bed at night. At first, I only made up prayers when I wanted something, like a prayer for loafer shoes instead of the same old oxfords or a prayer for a good report card. Then I realized it wasn't polite not to have thank-you prayers, too. Thank you, God, for my new shoes, and thank you for all S pluses on my report card.

Now, with my finger aching, I began to pray again.

The next thing I knew, I heard the flap of the window shade as Lyn pulled it up. It was morning, and I was still alive. I looked at my thumb. It was redder and fatter than any thumb had ever been in the history of fingers.

I couldn't even bend it. I got out of bed and went into the kitchen, where my mother was squeezing fresh orange juice.

"Look at this," I said, holding out my hand.

"Gerry! Where are your slippers?" my mother said automatically. "You'll catch a cold walking on the floor with bare feet."

"I already caught something," I said, showing my thumb to her.

She inspected the sore finger. "It looks like an ingrown nail," she said. "This is what happens when you bite your nails." But her voice wasn't angry. Ever since I was little I'd noticed that my mother had a very gentle tone with Lyn and me whenever we were ill.

"What will happen?" I asked.

"Here. Drink this before the vitamins go out of it," she said, handing me a glass of juice. "I'll make a solution of hot water and Epsom salts, and you'll have to soak your finger. It's filled with pus."

"Maybe now you'll finally stop biting your nails," my father said, when he saw my swollen finger. But he, too, spoke in a gentle tone.

Lyn went off to school, while I stayed home. Most of the time all the vitamins in the sunshine and orange juice seemed to work better in me than in Lyn. I had a practically perfect attendance record at school (except for Jewish holidays), but Lyn had several colds every winter. So it was unusual for me to be sitting alone in the quiet kitchen with my mother. Now that I knew I wasn't going to die I didn't feel so worried about my thumb. Anyhow, it is much less frightening to be sick in the daytime than in the middle of the night.

When the water in the teakettle boiled, my mother poured some into a bowl and added some Epsom salts. It was terribly hot, and I could hardly keep my thumb inside it. For the first second it felt freezing cold, and then it

began to burn. My mother added some cooler water, and gradually I was able to leave my finger in the bowl.

I watched my mother moving quietly around the kitchen, cleaning up the remains of our breakfast. "Mom," I asked, "do you believe in God?"

She turned to me and seemed to be considering her answer. Then she spoke. "No, I don't."

"I keep thinking about being Jewish," I said. "Edgar Wulf says that Jews have a responsibility to history. But we don't do anything to act Jewish, so it's hard for me to understand that responsibility." I paused a moment, and then I added, "But I do believe in God. I keep thinking about why I'm Jewish if I don't ever do anything to act Jewish," I repeated. "It doesn't make sense."

"Well," my mother explained, "according to Jewish law, anyone born of a Jewish mother is automatically Jewish. It's as simple as that."

"But there has to be more than that," I said. "There has to be a reason *why* I am Jewish. Something that I do or don't do. Not just because I'm alive."

"You'll understand better when you are older," my mother said to reassure me. But I disagreed.

"No, I'll understand less," I said. "If being a Jew is so complicated, then I should begin learning about it now so that I'll have more time for understanding. Maybe when I understand, then I won't believe in God anymore, just like you and Dad. But maybe I will. Maybe I'll learn to understand the chance that made me be born Jewish and Ann and Patty born Christian. We can still be friends, but I think it's important for me to know about my religion just as they know about theirs. I know more about their religion than I know about being Jewish."

I thought for a moment, and then I added, "Do you realize that I've gone to church with Ann and Patty several times? I went to the Christmas pageant that they put on, and we all went to Rita's wedding in the church last year, but I've never even stuck my toe into a synagogue."

"That's true," my mother agreed. "When we moved to this street, your father and I didn't know that there were so few Jewish families in the immediate neighborhood. And even when we realized, we were pleased that you could grow up here. For centuries, Jews have been forced to live together in tight ghetto communities. It's good to live in a mixed neighborhood so that people can learn about one another, just as you have learned about Ann and Patty. That's the secret of understanding."

"Yes," I said, "I've learned about *them*, but what have I learned about *myself*? And what have they learned about me? I'm not Catholic and I'm not Protestant, like some of the kids at school, and I'm not really Jewish either. Patty thinks I'm a Communist," I said, looking at my mother. Lately that word was heard more and more on the news, and it was about the worst thing you could say about a person. "I'm a nothing," I said. "It confuses my friends and it confuses me!"

"You can't expect us to start observing Jewish holidays just so your Christian friends can learn about Judaism," my mother said, and laughed. "Your father and I prefer making our own holidays and our own regulations for good behavior and not following rules that we feel have no meaning for us in 1948. And we enjoy living here where we can act as we wish. No one cares if we are Jewish or not."

I thought about the swastika on the mailbox. I wondered what my mother had thought the first time she had seen it. And I wondered if she was aware that Dad was the one who was drawing over it every week so that we could pretend it wasn't there.

The doorbell rang. It was Mrs. D'Amato wanting to use the telephone. She often used ours instead of walking up to the corner to use the one at the candy store. She examined my finger and exclaimed, "My grandmother used to make a poultice of brown bread and brown paper!" She paused and thought. "No, maybe it was brown bread and brown soap. I don't remember."

"We could try all three," my mother said.

"Do I have to eat brown bread and brown soap and brown paper?" I gagged at the thought. It sounded awful.

"Not to eat. To put on your thumb and draw out the infection," Mrs. D'Amato explained. She took off her coat and reached under the sink where we kept our brown soap, and she began cutting a little of it into a dish. My mother handed her a slice of pumpernickel bread and a paper bag. In a few minutes there was a gooey mess sticking to my finger. It didn't hurt, but it did look revolting.

"Oh, how late it's getting," said Mrs. D'Amato, looking at the kitchen clock. She made her phone call and left, promising to return later in the day to inspect my finger.

My mother went to the door with her. When she returned, she said, "Mrs. D'Amato is a wonderful woman, and it is very important to me that we have good friends of all religions. Someday, if you become an observant Jew, or even if you adopt another religion, just remember that. Don't let religion be a reason to separate you from other people. Too many people have been killed in this world because of religion. If there is a God, I'm certain of one thing—this was not his plan for the universe. Religion should teach people how to love one another and how to live better lives, but so far it only seems to have taught people to hate."

I thought about what my mother said, and afterward I didn't want to mention the business of the swastika on the mailbox. Instead, we spoke of other, less serious things. Then I turned on the radio and spent most of the afternoon listening to soap operas. They were very interesting and the only bad thing was that I would be in school the next day and would never know how all the problems had been solved.

By the time Lyn returned from school, my finger was much better. I didn't know which cure had worked—the hot water or the poultice. When my father came home from work, he brought me a small manicure kit that he had found in a shop near the post office. He said he hoped it would encourage me to take better care of my nails.

"I'll try," I said, and I made a quiet little prayer inside myself to God that he would remind me whenever a finger found its way into my mouth.

8
Girl Scouts

One evening, about a week later, my mother received a telephone call. When she got off the phone she announced that she had wonderful news for me. Something in her tone gave me doubts, even before I heard what the news was.

Lyn, who as usual couldn't bear to miss out on anything, began to whine, "I want good news too."

My mother ignored her and said to me, "That was Mrs. Shapiro. She called to say that there is an opening in the Girl Scout troop and that they would love to have you become a member."

Instantly I had a picture in my head of how I would look wearing a green uniform with the little colored patches sewn on the sleeve.

Then I started thinking of the other girls who wore Girl Scout uniforms to school on Wednesday, which was the meeting day. I didn't like any of them.

"Can Ann and Patty come with me?" I asked.

"There is only one opening just now, and I put your name on the waiting list months ago. Maybe their mothers will sign them up, and eventually they can join too. Anyway, it will be nice for you to make some new friends besides the children on this street," she said.

"Do I *have* to become a Girl Scout?" I asked. I was thinking of Sheila Shapiro and Lois Weiss, who were both in the troop. They were not among my favorite people, even if I was curious about them.

"It's a wonderful opportunity," my mother answered. "You'll love it."

From the second I walked into the meeting hall on the following Wednesday, I knew I wouldn't love it. It's strange to be in a room that you know very well and still to be in it for the first time. The Girl Scouts met in the very same American Legion Hall where I used to take modern-dance lessons on Saturday mornings. I used to lie on the floor stretching my leg muscles and getting dirty and picking up splinters once a week for almost a year. My mother had heard about Miss Matty, who was trying to support herself giving lessons, and I had to go. Then Miss Matty moved away, and the lessons stopped.

Now it was a Wednesday afternoon, and because the room was filled with different people, I felt as if I had never been there before. I was very uncomfortable. All the girls were in their uniforms. Even Mrs. Shapiro wore a green sash over her dress to show that she was the leader. In my red corduroy jumper and white blouse, I felt odd and out of place among the green-clothed girls.

Mrs. Shapiro noticed me and walked in my

direction. "Welcome to our troop," she said. "The Girl Scouts are a national organization. We are nonsectarian, and we are pleased to have you join us. Because I started this troop among my daughter's friends, until today all our members have been Jewish. So we are especially proud to have a Christian girl join our ranks."

For a moment I was confused. Then I realized that Mrs. Shapiro was talking about me. I was usually at a loss when someone asked me what I was. If I said I was American, they always asked, "Yes, but what else?" I was never eager to admit that I was Jewish whether a Christian or a Jewish person was questioning me because I was such a nothing. But now I felt that I had to correct Mrs. Shapiro's misconception about me. Maybe the reason that I was invited into the troop was because they needed to have a Christian member.

"I'm not Christian," I said. "I'm Jewish too."

"You are?" Mrs. Shapiro looked at me, incredulously.

I nodded my head. It's true that we didn't keep kosher or pray or anything. But still in all, I was Jewish.

"Oh, that is wonderful," said Mrs. Shapiro, beaming at me. "Then you really are one of us!"

I didn't feel as though I was one of them when I sat in the circle on the floor and saw Lois Weiss looking at me and then nudging her neighbor and giggling. Mrs. Shapiro introduced me to the girls. She had several announcements to make. They were going to make Easter baskets and take them to the children at Morrisania Hospital. That started me thinking. I wondered if God was happy that all these Jewish girls were going to make Easter baskets.

Mrs. Shapiro spoke about a trip that the Girl Scouts might take in a few weeks. Then

she started singing, and all the girls joined in. I didn't know any of the words, and I couldn't decide if I should move my lips and pretend to be singing or just sit there with my mouth closed. I loved to sing, but in school I was a whisperer. That meant I was not allowed to sing but could only whisper when we had music because my voice was so bad. Every year at Christmastime, many of the Jewish students brought in notes from their parents explaining that singing the holiday carols was against their religion. But since I wasn't permitted to sing out loud anyway, I never asked my mother for a note. Besides, my parents probably would say, "go ahead and sing." I wondered what the Girl Scout policy was about singing.

Then Mrs. Shapiro said that we could have a free-play period. "Hide and seek! Let's play hide and seek!" everyone shouted. Immediately they began calling out "Not it!" Luckily, one of the girls must have wanted to be it because she deliberately waited to call out last, and even I managed to call out before her. We all ran to hide while the counting began.

First I thought I would hide inside the little closet where Miss Matty used to store her drum and mat after dance class last year. But it was locked, and so I got another idea. I climbed onto the table in the back of the room where all the girls had piled their coats. I crawled under the coats and held my breath. It was a good hiding place. All around me I could hear the whispers of the other girls as they crouched in various corners or behind pillars in the room or inside the phone booth in the back.

"Ready or not, here I come," called the girl who was it. I knew her from school. She was in the sixth grade and very bossy. She'll never find me, I thought, pleased with my cleverness.

There was the sound of running as someone

jumped out of the phone booth and hurried to make it back to home free. There were shouts as someone else was discovered in her hiding place. One by one, each of the girls was found. I waited under the heavy pile of clothing. I didn't care if I was found now, because at least I wouldn't be it if we played another round. I peeked out to see if I should run to home base. The girls were all sitting on the floor in a circle and beginning a new game. They didn't even know that I was still hiding. They had forgotten that I was a part of their troop.

I tried to decide if I should just emerge from the cocoon of coats. What would I say? "Ha, ha, you couldn't find me." Or I could just go and quietly join the other girls in the circle. But I didn't know what game they were playing, and I didn't know the rules. Besides, maybe they hadn't looked for me because they didn't want to find me.

I heard the voice of Mrs. Shapiro saying,

"All right, Judy. You be the first." Even Mrs. Shapiro had forgotten about me. I could stay hidden under the coats all afternoon, and no one would know. "I'll count to ten and then I'll walk out," I promised myself, chewing on one of my nails. I began counting slowly, but by the time I reached seven I realized that I was not planning to leave my hiding place.

"If they don't want to play with me, then I'll stay right here," I told myself. It was hot and stuffy under the coats as I sniffed back some tears. Maybe I'd suffocate to death, then they'd be sorry.

I began to wonder what I would say to my mother when she asked about the meeting. Perhaps I could convince her that since all we did was play some games, there was nothing very special about the Scouts. Maybe she wouldn't make me return next week.

I heard running feet. The meeting was finally over. The girls were all coming to get their coats. I slid out from under them and made a big show of looking for my brown coat among all the others. I was feeling stiff from remaining in one position for so long. No one seemed surprised to see me. No one asked, "Where were you?" And no one said, "Good-bye," as I rushed out the door without even buttoning my coat.

Lyn was waiting inside the apartment door when I got home. "Was it fun? Could I go with you sometime? You're so lucky. It isn't fair," she said, the words all rushing out together.

I wasn't going to tell her that I didn't like being a Girl Scout. "It was loads of fun," I lied. "But you wouldn't like it. Girl Scouts is just for big girls," I said with superiority. At least for the moment, seeing Lyn's envy, I could feel important.

"I had a wonderful time," I stressed. But even as I spoke, I was racking my brain trying to think of a good excuse for not going back to Girl Scouts the following week.

Of course I went back. When my mother made up her mind about something, it was very hard to make her change it. I consoled myself with the thought of the uniform. I would have it in another week. At least, every Wednesday Lois Weiss couldn't laugh at my dresses with the worn creases showing from the previous hems. Wednesdays, we would look alike.

Both Ann and Patty pretended that they weren't interested in the Girl Scouts, but I knew that they envied me. "We're going to march in a parade," I boasted. I had missed out on the Columbus Day parade in October, but in May the troop would be marching on the Grand Concourse to celebrate Decoration Day. That would be something!

"Maybe it will rain," said Patty, shrugging her shoulders. What she really meant was that she wished she could march in a parade too.

9
Embarrassments and Worse

Now that I was taking piano lessons and in the Girl Scouts, I didn't seem to spend as much time out on the stoop. But on Mondays I didn't have to go anywhere. So there I was sitting outside after school together with Ann and Patty. It was almost spring, and the weather was quite warm. Soon we would be able to go to the park again.

None of us felt like playing ball or jumping rope. We just sat watching Lyn and a couple of little kids playing roly-poly. They looked so babyish that it was hard to remember that only last year we still played that game. All our old games like 10-A's, Red Light-Green Light, and Giant Steps were becoming dull. My mother said we were growing up. It's always like that, she told me. But not for the boys on our block. They never seemed to get tired of stickball. Even the fathers joined in playing the game on summer evenings.

"What is the most embarrassing thing that ever happened to you?" asked Ann, breaking the silence.

Patty started giggling. "It was when I was in church and I gave a very strong sneeze, and my nose started bleeding. It was dripping blood right on the floor."

"That's nothing," said Ann. "My sister, Rita, knows a girl who was bleeding on the floor, and it wasn't from her *nose!*" She spoke with authority. Having a big sister, Ann knew lots of things that Patty and I didn't. She was the one who first told us that when we grew up we would start bleeding and need to use Colgates every month. Another year went by before my mother explained what would happen to me. (Anyhow, Ann got it all confused. Colgates is toothpaste.)

"Well, what about you?" asked Patty.

"Oh," began Ann dramatically. Then she told us about how she had eaten a big dinner and then thrown up all over her aunt's new carpet when she was little.

"Those may be embarrassing things," I agreed, "but you were both sick. And you can't help it when you are sick." I thought of all the times that I felt awkward and embarrassed, not because I was sick, but because I was me, Geraldine Flam. I was embarrassed every single Sunday when I sat out on the stoop waiting for my friends to come home from church.

But then I remembered something that happened just the week before. My mother had arranged for me to go and play with Marsha Schwartz. She was in the Girl Scout troop with me, and my mother often spoke with her mother in the park. Anyhow, the visit was all planned by our mothers, and Marsha and I didn't have anything to say about it. Even so, I half wanted to go. Marsha was one of the few people I knew of who had a television set. I had never seen one except in the advertisements in the newspaper. They cost about four hundred dollars, and it could probably be four hundred years before we could get one.

We watched a program called "Howdy Doody," which was like a puppet show. It was just like a movie in your own home except that the picture was much smaller. The screen on the television was ten inches. Marsha said most of the programs were either news or sports. She said she watched a lot of wrestling matches, and boxing too.

Then Marsha asked me if I wanted some ice cream.

"If you do," I said, hoping she would say she did.

It was chocolate, a whole large container of

it, and we helped ourselves to big bowls. I got the spoons out of the kitchen drawer while she got the dishes. We were eating when Mrs. Schwartz came into the kitchen.

"Marsha, what are you doing?" she shrieked, as she came nearer to the table where we were sitting. I thought she was angry because we were eating ice cream and it was close to suppertime. But then she said, "You are eating ice cream with meat spoons!" It was the funniest thing I had ever heard. Who uses spoons to eat meat? I started to giggle. I had visions of Marsha and her parents sitting down to lamb chops and trying to eat them with a spoon. My giggles got louder and louder, and then I was laughing so hard that tears were pouring out of my eyes.

"What is the matter with you?" yelled Marsha's mother. "How can I use these spoons again?"

"Can't you wash the ice cream off?" I asked, when I finally caught my breath.

"They won't be kosher. We can't use these spoons."

The laughter stuck in my throat. I was so stupid. I had forgotten that many religious Jews use separate silverware and dishes for meat meals and for milk meals. "I was so embarrassed that I thought I would die, and I couldn't wait to go home," I explained now to Ann and Patty. "Why hadn't Marsha noticed and stopped me when I took the wrong spoons out of the drawer?"

"Meat spoons!" They were both laughing. "What a silly religion you belong to. Meat spoons!" They shouted the words for all the block to hear.

"How come you don't have meat spoons in your house?" Patty asked me.

"Yeah, what kind of a Jew are you anyhow?" asked Ann. "If we were supposed to have meat spoons, we would have them. Meat spoons. Jews have meat spoons!" Ann laughed again. "Maybe they grind up their meat and make it mushy like baby food."

"Meat spoons!"

Suddenly as Ann and Patty laughed at me, I was just as embarrassed on my own stoop as I had been in Marsha's apartment on the Grand Concourse.

A little later we all went indoors. I started to do my homework, but I had something in my eye and it hurt badly. My mother tried to get it out, but she wasn't successful. "You'd better go over to the drugstore and see if Mr. Crane can get it out for you," she said. So I put my coat back on and went around the corner to the pharmacy. Taking a stick with a piece of cotton on it, Mr. Crane removed the cinder from my eye in a moment.

As I left the drugstore, I saw Edgar walking just ahead of me.

"Hi!" I called out, skipping to catch up with him. I'd been over to his house a few times by then, working on my stamp collection with him. "You're awfully late from school," I said.

"We're starting a chess club," he explained.

Just as we reached the corner of our street, we were blocked by a group of boys coming out of the candy store. The boys stood so they were taking up the entire sidewalk, making it impossible to pass.

"Excuse us, please," said Edgar. His voice sounded forced and unnatural.

"*Achtung!*" said one of the boys. He was Paul D'Amato. "*Heil* Hitler!" he said, and he raised his arm in a German-style salute.

"*Heil Hitler!*" shouted all the boys together, and their arms went up in the air too.

Edgar's face turned a bright red, and he didn't say anything. This would count as an embarrassing moment for him, I guessed.

"Hey, come on, Paulie, let us pass," I said. "I've got to get home."

"You Jews sure stick together, don't you?" said Eddie, another of the boys. "You Christ-killers don't belong around here."

A sudden feeling of nausea swept over me. They weren't just taunting Edgar. They were taunting me, too. My father was right when he said that even here in the Bronx there were people who didn't like Jews. For a moment I wondered if Eddie was the one who had scratched the swastika on the mailbox, but of course he couldn't have. When it was done years ago, he was too young and too short to have been able to.

One of the boys spit at Edgar and me. "Why don't you go back where you came from!"

"I was born here!" I shouted at him. "I belong in the Bronx just as much as you do. I'm an American."

"Come on, fellas," said Paul D'Amato. "Let's go over to the school yard and play."

The boys followed his lead and turned to cross the street. They no longer paid any attention to Edgar and me. I didn't know what to say to Edgar. He seemed very upset.

"They were just fooling around," I said to reassure him, and to reassure myself, too.

"Someday," said Edgar, "when the Jews have their own homeland, people won't be able to act that way anymore."

"Well, it just doesn't make sense," I complained to him. "This is my homeland." I thought of the words that had been shouted at us. "And I never killed anyone. I never would."

Edgar explained to me what the boys had meant. "According to the Christian Bible, the man who betrayed Jesus Christ was a Jew. So Jews have often been referred to as murderers."

"I never knew that," I said.

"Here's something else you probably didn't

132

know," said Edgar. "Did you know that Jesus Christ was Jewish?"

It was strange that Ann and Patty had never told me that!

The incident with Paul and his friends was so unpleasant that thinking about it brought tears to my eyes. The tears were not from the eye irritation of ten minutes before. Like the cinder that Mr. Crane had removed, there was something very small and sharp inside me that pained deeply, more than one would suspect from the size of it.

10
Easter Shopping

Easter was in March that year, but Ann and Patty had been talking about it for weeks before it came. They started on Ash Wednesday, which was sometime in February, when they went to St. Angela's Church and the priest made a cross on their forehead with burned palm ashes. Actually, the cross looked just like a smudge. Once, when I was about eight years old and I saw my friends with their smudged foreheads, I put some dirt on my head so I would look just like them. "Oh, that's a sacrilege," said Patty. I didn't know what a sacrilege was, but it sounded pretty terrible.

Now that I knew, it seemed to me that my family had committed many actions that were in contempt of God. "Those are the worst sins of all," said Ann. My family's behavior on Easter was a sacrilege. Every year on Easter Sunday, Ann and Patty and the other kids on the street wore new spring outfits. Their mothers bought them all new clothing, and it was worn for the first time on the holiday. My mother wanted Lyn and me to have new spring clothing too. And so she also bought us clothes, which, regardless of the weather, we wore for the first time on Easter Sunday.

One year when Ann was angry at me for something or other, she saw my new clothes and said, "Why are you all dressed up? It isn't *your* holiday."

My answer was, "It's a free country. I can do what I want." I think she was jealous because my outfit was prettier than hers, but in a way she was right.

Most years, however, things passed quietly. Lyn and I sat outside on the stoop, waiting till Ann and Patty returned from church with their families. Both Lyn and I had elaborate Easter baskets with chocolate and sugar eggs as well as the hard-boiled eggs that we dyed various colors. After church we all sat around and compared the contents of our baskets and traded with one another. Sometimes we reminisced about the Easter during the war when there weren't enough eggs for coloring. But that year, on the day before Easter, there was a rainbow in the sky. It was the first one I had ever seen. Everyone looked at it from their windows and said it was a miracle of God, that he was giving us all the colors in the sky since we couldn't have the colored eggs.

On the Monday after Easter, my father brought home a small glass prism, which he hung in the window of Lyn's and my bedroom so it made a rainbow on the wall, and he tried to explain to us about refraction of light and why we saw the colors in the sky and on the wall. He said there was a scientific reason for it, but I liked the idea of the miracle better.

This year, ever since Paul had stopped Edgar and me on the street and accused us of killing Jesus, I had been feeling uncomfortable. And now I certainly didn't want to celebrate Easter, which is a holiday marking the death and resurrection of Jesus Christ. (I looked up *resurrection* in the dictionary, and it means rising from the dead. That's a *real* miracle!)

My mother had planned to go shopping for new clothes with Lyn and me after school on Monday, but it was raining hard and she decided to postpone it. We always did our shopping on 149th Street and Third Avenue. There were many big stores there, and we usually had to try them all until we found what she liked or what fit me. Since Tuesday and Thursday afternoons were piano lessons, and Wednesday afternoon was the Girl Scout meeting, we couldn't go until Friday. By Thursday morning, Lyn had another of her bad colds and my mother knew that she couldn't take her shopping on Friday afternoon. So instead, she decided that just the two of us would go on Thursday evening when the stores stayed open late and my father would be home to take care of Lyn.

After depositing our nickels in the coin box, we took our seats on the bus. I was pleased to be going for new clothes, and I was glad to shop at night, which seemed very grown-up. But I also felt a great unhappiness about the coming holiday.

"Doesn't it seem strange to buy clothes for a Christian celebration?" I asked my mother.

"Well, first of all, you do need new shoes for the spring. Nothing fits you anymore. You have to wear something on your feet, and that has nothing whatsoever to do with any religion."

138

My mother was right there. Nobody of any religion had feet as big as I did. Here I was, not even eleven, and already I wore size eight shoes. If I kept on growing, by the time I was sixteen, I was going to have feet that were size sixteen too! The men in the shoe departments always thought my feet were a big joke. "We'll be glad to sell you the boxes," they said, when the contents of the boxes pinched my toes.

"Well, this year, let's not call them my Easter shoes when I get them," I said. "It sounds stupid."

"Actually," said my mother, "you'll have another opportunity for dressing up in your Easter clothes, if you want it."

"What's that?" I asked with trepidation. Ever since I was pushed into becoming a Girl Scout, I'd been suspicious about the plans that my mother made for me.

"Mrs. Wulf spoke to me and invited us all to have a seder with them in April at Passover.

I explained that we didn't observe the holiday. But I'm sure she would be pleased if you want to attend. Would you like to go?"

"What is a seder?" I asked.

"It's a big dinner that Jews have in the spring," my mother said. "My aunt Rose used to have one when I was a child. They read the story of how the Jews were slaves in Egypt, and they eat a lot of symbolic food like hardboiled eggs and matzohs. You'd probably find it very interesting."

"I didn't know the Jews were slaves," I said. "Did Abraham Lincoln free them too?"

"There are a lot of things you don't know," my mother said. "Maybe your father and I have been wrong not to give you any Jewish identity. I'll call Mrs. Wulf and tell her that you and Lyn will come to her seder. That will make you feel more Jewish," she added.

"Was Lyn invited too?" I liked to think that I had become a special friend of the Wulf family. Ann and Patty had begun teasing me

that Edgar was my boyfriend. I didn't feel romantic about him at all. He was an interesting person, but I didn't want to marry him. He looked even less like Cornell Wilde than Paul D'Amato did.

"Of course the invitation included Lyn," my mother said.

For a moment I felt annoyed. Why did Lyn have to come along to the Wulfs' dinner with me? Then I started thinking about it. After all, Lyn was just as Jewish or un-Jewish as I was, even though she was too young to have started thinking about it yet. When I was seven I didn't think about why I was different from the others. It didn't bother me then that I was a nothing. But soon she would begin to feel the same emptiness that I felt. I was glad that she was coming. We could learn about the seder together.

"Here's our stop," said my mother, and she grabbed my hand.

We got off the bus and started a tour of the shoe stores. It was a good thing that Lyn wasn't with us. We went to six different stores before I was able to find a pair of shoes and not boxes to fit my feet. But for once I didn't complain as my mother dragged me from shop to shop. I patiently tried on shoes and looked at the X rays of my toes in each store. I would wear my new shoes when I went to celebrate the Passover holiday with the Wulfs. It would be an important night in my life.

11
A Long Night in April

I looked forward to the seder ceremony at the Wulfs' with mixed feelings. I was glad that I was going, but I was a little scared, too. I didn't know what I was supposed to say or do. As a result, I was very glad that Lyn was coming with me. She didn't know anything about the Passover holiday either, which was a comfort.

On the evening of the seder, my mother supervised as we both got dressed. She checked that the part in my hair was straight, and she helped button the back of my dress. Then she put her hand in her pocket and pulled something out. "My aunt Rose gave this to me when I was about your age. I never wore it much, but it seemed bad luck to throw it away. You can have it if you want. It seems to mean more to you than it ever did to me."

She opened her hand and inside was a tiny six-pointed star on a chain. She helped me put it on.

Against the ruffled front of my dress I could hardly see it. But it made me feel good to know it was there. I gave my mother a thank-you hug. "Now I feel really Jewish," I said.

I called to Lyn. It was time for us to go.

At the Wulfs', Lyn and I were given seats, side by side, around a large table that had been set up in the living room. In addition to Edgar and his parents, there were an elderly aunt and uncle of Mr. Wulf's, Fanny and Max, and another old woman, also a relative. She was Aunt Elsie. At each place there was a little book with the story of the Passover. It was called the Haggadah.

I had taken a book out of the library and

146

read a little about the holiday so I wouldn't be in total ignorance. I thought it was interesting, and I wondered why it had never occurred to me in the past to read about the Jewish holidays and customs. I decided that I would read about them all and also read the stories of the Old Testament. That is the Jewish Bible, and Ann and Patty both knew more about it than I did. Yet even though I had studied about Passover, I was nervous as if I had been preparing for a test at school. I didn't want to make a fool out of myself.

Everything on the table looked strange. There were many unusual foods spread about: a plate with matzohs, parsley, horseradish, a bone, and hard-boiled eggs. There was a bowl of salt water to remind one of tears, and there was a mixture of apples and nuts and wine that was supposed to look like the mortar used by the Jewish slaves in Egypt when they made bricks. The meal would be most peculiar. I began to wish that I were back in my own apartment eating the meat loaf with a hard-boiled egg in the center and the baked potatoes that had been cooking in the oven when I left.

Under the table, Lyn grabbed hold of my hand. Obviously she, too, had second thoughts about sitting at this strange table. She probably felt worse than I did. After all, she hardly knew Mrs. Wulf at all, and she hadn't done any studying about the Passover seder. I squeezed her hand sympathetically. We were both outsiders at this affair.

"Don't worry," I whispered softly in her ear.

The seder began. Mr. Wulf washed his hands in a bowl of water that his wife gave him. "Is the sink broken?" Lyn asked me.

Then Mr. Wulf picked up the little book from beside his plate and began to read. He read rapidly, and the words made no sense

because they were in Hebrew. Luckily, there was a translation on the opposite side of each page. Mr. Wulf paused and asked Edgar to go on with the reading. He read in Hebrew too, chanting the words to a melody. Then it was time to take a drink of wine. I took the tiniest of sips. It was the very first time Lyn and I had ever been given wine to drink. It wasn't bad, but Lyn made a face.

Mrs. Wulf noticed. "Wait," she said. "Let me get the grape juice. I bought it especially for you."

"No, thank you," said Lyn in a small voice. "I want to go home. Gerry, let's go home," she said, pulling at my arm.

It was a chance to escape. I could say good-bye and leave. When I next saw Mrs. Wulf at my piano lesson, I could blame our leaving on Lyn. After all, she was only seven years old. I looked around the table. Everyone was looking at us. Edgar and his father looked very serious, both of them wearing little black skullcaps on their heads. Aunt Fanny and Aunt Elsie and Uncle Max were looking too. Their faces were lined with wrinkles. They had come here many years before. Without their help, Edgar and his parents would have been killed by the Nazis as his other relatives were. Aunt Elsie smiled at Lyn. "Come, sit on my lap," she said. "Before you know it will be dinner time."

Lyn shook her head. "I want to go home," she said again, and she began to cry.

"Let me take her," I said. "It was very nice of you to ask us, but we're not very Jewish, and this is awfully strange for her. We've never done anything like it before."

"I understand," said Mr. Wulf. He got up from the table and brought us our jackets.

I walked out of the house with Lyn. It was a wonderful relief to leave the seder. Outside it had grown dark, and the streetlamps were on. My jacket was unbuttoned, and I looked down at my new Easter dress. The light shone on the tiny star resting on my chest. I had forgotten it was there.

"Lyn," I said suddenly, "do you mind if I go back after I take you home? Then I'll be able to tell you all about it. Maybe next year we can have a seder at our own house when we understand it better. I think we should know about being Jews. I think it's important."

Lyn nodded in agreement and wiped her nose with the back of her hand.

So I returned to the Wulfs' apartment after all. Everyone seemed happy to see me.

"I thought it was too early for Elijah," said Mr. Wulf, when he opened the door in response to my ring.

They all smiled at me so much that I felt very good and as if I really belonged with them.

"Would you like a turn to read?" Mr. Wulf asked me.

"I can't read Hebrew," I said, blushing.

"So read the English," he said. "That's a good language too. When I was a child, I used to read in German until I learned the Hebrew."

I read slowly, pausing at all the proper places and using lots of expression, the way I learned at school.

> In every generation one must look upon himself as if he personally had come out from Egypt, as the Bible says: "And thou shalt tell thy son on that day, saying, it is because of that which the Eternal did to me when I went forth from Egypt." For it was not alone our forefathers whom the Holy One, blessed be He, redeemed; He redeemed us too, with them, as it is said: "He brought us out from there that He might lead us to and give us the land which He pledged to our forefathers."

The seder continued with more reading. The various food items on the table were passed around. I took tiny bites of everything, even the bitter herbs. When the time came for the real meal, I was surprised at how good it was. I had thought we would eat only herbs and other symbolic foods. But Mrs. Wulf served chicken soup with matzoh balls, which my mother made sometimes too. Then there was roast chicken and potatoes and something called *tzimmes,* which had carrots and prunes and meat all cooked together.

Everyone drank a lot of sweet wine and sang many Passover songs. Aunt Fanny and Uncle Max had terrible, scratchy voices, worse than any of the whisperers in my class at school. But they sang loudly and no one objected. One song had so many verses that, by the end of it, I was able to join in too, because I caught on to the melody and the English words were printed in the Haggadah.

"Good for you, Gerry. I like to hear you sing," said Mr. Wulf.

No one had ever said that to me before!

"This is one of the most special Passovers

in the history of the Jewish people," Mr. Wulf said to me. "I'm very glad that you were able to spend it with us. Each year during the seder we say, 'Next year in Jerusalem,' and now, in 1948, these words can take on a new meaning. There aren't enough Jews left in the world, but for those of us who are here it is a wonderful thing to know we have our own country at last. We must be proud and help keep the new Jewish state alive and strong."

I knew he was talking about Palestine. It was still hard for me to understand the concept of a whole country with only Jewish people living in it. I would have to try and read my father's newspapers and listen to the news broadcasts on the radio more carefully so that I could understand it better.

When the seder was over, Edgar offered to walk me home.

"That's silly!" I laughed. "I can't get lost going to the next building. I only took Lyn home because she is still so little."

Mrs. Wulf handed me a paper bag with some macaroon cookies inside. "These are for your sister," she said, smiling. "Maybe next year she will be big enough to stay up for the whole seder."

"Next year I'll teach you how to ask the four questions in Hebrew," Edgar promised.

I said good night to Mr. Wulf and Aunt Fanny and Aunt Elsie and Uncle Max, who were still sitting around the dinner table drinking cups of tea. On a sudden impulse, I hugged Mrs. Wulf and gave her a kiss. Imagine that I had once been so stupid as to think that she was interested in chopping up children.

"Look what my mother gave me," I said, showing her the little star around my neck. "It was hers when she was my age. It really makes me feel Jewish now."

"It's lovely," said Mrs. Wulf. "But you know, even if you don't wear it you will still always be Jewish. Just the way the stars are up in the sky even in the daylight when we can't see them. And you have always had that star even when you couldn't see it and show it to me."

It's funny that I had never thought about stars being in the sky in the daytime.

I ran down the steps of the building and stood for a minute in the street. There was not another soul about. The air was cold and smelled fresh after the stuffiness of the Wulfs' apartment. For some reason, I felt important standing there, the only person on the street. I looked up and saw the full moon and the sky filled with stars, and I remembered the night so long ago when I had sat outside waiting for my own special star to fall to the ground. I felt the chain around my neck with the little star on it. Tonight I had actually gotten my star. But Mrs. Wulf was right; the star wasn't so important. It was much more important that I had acted like a Jew for the first time in my life. At the very moment that I had sat at the Wulfs' table, thousands and thousands of Jews throughout the world were also sitting and reading the Haggadah together. I was part of a long, invisible chain, a chain that was stronger than the little one around my neck.

I wondered if God was up in the sky looking down at me now, as Ann and Patty always insisted that he was. There was still so much that I didn't know or understand.

I heard some shuffling footsteps and saw a familiar figure coming down the street in my direction. It was Mrs. Wallace, taking Willie out for her evening walk. "What are you doing out so late?" she asked, when she recognized me. Then without even waiting for an answer, she said, "How are you? You are lucky. You could be blind. Or just imagine that you were deaf and dumb. Be glad that you are you."

I bent down and gave Willie the customary pat.

Then I stood up and smiled at Mrs. Wallace in the dark.

"Oh, Mrs. Wallace," I said, "I am glad that I am me."

And for once I really meant it.